POLAR BEARS

Written and edited by **Lucy Baker**

Consultant Doug Richardson, Head Keeper,
Mappin Terraces, London Zoo

PUFFIN BOOKS

PUFFIN BOOKS
Published by the Penguin Group
Viking Penguin, a division of Penguin Books USA Inc.,
40 West 23rd Street, New York, New York 10010, U.S.A.

First published in Great Britain by Two-Can Publishing Ltd., 1990

First American edition published in Puffin Books, 1990

1 3 5 7 9 10 8 6 4 2

Copyright © Two-Can Publishing Ltd., 1990

Text copyright © Lucy Baker, 1990

All rights reserved

ISBN 0-14-034435-7

Printed in Portugal

Photograhic Credits:
Front cover Bruce Coleman p.4-5 B. & C. Alexander p.6 B. & C. Alexander/Bruce Coleman p.7 C. Carvalho/Frank Lane Picture Agency p.8-9 Tom Ulrich/Oxford Scientific
Films p.11 top B. & C. Alexander bottom Thor Larsen/Bruce Coleman p.12 Margot Conte/Oxford Scientific Films p.13 Leonard Lee Rue III/Bruce Coleman p.14 B. & C.
Alexander p.15 top Wayne Lankinen/Bruce Coleman bottom Leonard Lee Rue III/Bruce Coleman p.16 B. & C. Alexander p.17 top Tony Martin/Oxford Scientific Films
bottom B. & C. Alexander p.18 John E. Nees/Oxford Scientific Films p.19 B. & C. Alexander

Illustration Credits:
p.4-19 David Cook/Linden Artists p.20-21 Chris Rothero/Linden Artists p.24-25 Malcolm Livingstone p.26-30 Graeme Corbett p.31 Alan Rogers

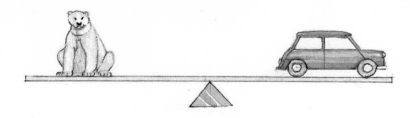

CONTENTS

LOOKING AT POLAR BEARS

Polar bears are very large. They are more than twice the size of lions and tigers. They live around the North Pole in an area called the Arctic.

The Eskimo people, or Inuit, who live in the Arctic call the polar bear *Nanook*, which means great white bear. Sometimes hungry or curious bears raid Inuit villages. The Inuit hunt polar bears for food and clothing.

Polar bears are covered in thick fur which can be very white or a golden yellow color. They have shiny black noses and small dark eyes. Polar bears' legs are very short, but they have long necks and huge rumps.

When hungry, polar bears can be very dangerous. They have been known to attack and kill people.

POLAR BEAR FACTS

Big polar bears can weigh as much as a small car.

The biggest polar bears stand over three meters (11 feet) tall.

◀ Polar bears lie down to sleep or to avoid the cold Arctic wind. They roll on the icy ground to dry themselves after swimming.

▶ When polar bears are approached in the wild, they rarely run away, nor are they aggressive or fierce like their cousins the grizzly bears. They hold their ground – proud and bold. When a polar bear stands upright, it could look an elephant in the eye!

THE POLAR BEARS' HOME

Long ago, people believed that the Arctic was the end of the world. It is certainly a cold, icy wilderness.

Much of the Arctic is not land at all, but ocean. Ice covers the Arctic waters for most of the year. Huge chunks of ice collide and form enormous floating islands called pack ice. Polar bears spend most of their lives on the pack ice, hunting for seals.

The Arctic is a very quiet place. The silence is broken only occasionally, perhaps by a lone bird call or by the cracking of ice. The only landmarks in the Arctic are towering icebergs and mysterious pools of water that never freeze. No one knows how polar bears find their way around their icy home, but they always seem to know where they are going and the best way to get there.

In winter the Arctic is extremely cold. For weeks the sun never rises and it is dark right through the day. The polar bears' thick layers of fat help to protect them from the cold. Their thick, white coats are made of special hairs. Each hair is a tiny, hollow tube that carries the sun's warmth down to their bodies.

Many polar bears stay in one area of the Arctic all their lives, but some travel thousands of kilometers over huge ice mountains and across large stretches of icy water. On flat ground, polar bears can travel up to 56 kilometers (35 miles) an hour, but only for very short lengths of time.

◄ Polar bears often travel great distances across the Arctic wilderness. Most bears stay near their home ground, but some wander hundreds of kilometers.

▲ Polar bears are good swimmers and can swim for hours at a time. Their feet are partially webbed to help them move through the water.

POLAR BEAR FACTS

When polar bears swim, they use their front paws like oars.

Polar bears walk on all fours, moving both left feet forward and then both right feet – you try it!

Polar bears can swim underwater. They flatten their ears and close their nostrils, but keep their eyes open.

LIFE IN THE ARCTIC

Spring is a good time for polar bears. Hundreds of seals are born in holes under the pack ice, and polar bears spend their days hunting the seals for food.

In the summer, the pack ice melts and the polar bears are forced ashore. Away from their hunting grounds, polar bears survive by eating seaweed, berries, grasses and small birds and animals.

▶ People used to believe that polar bears were solitary animals that did not like company. In fact, they sometimes travel together and large males spend hours engaged in mock battles with their friends. It is only when polar bears are hunting that they need to be alone.

Polar bears may travel far inland during the summer months. They have been seen 160 kilometers (100 miles) from the sea. As winter approaches, they return to the shore. Every day they check to see if the water has frozen. As soon as the ice is thick enough, the bears leave. They are hungry and want to catch and eat as many seals as they can before the bitter winter begins.

To shelter from the winter blizzards, polar bears dig caves in the snow. Some stay inside for months, others only weeks or days. Hungry bears continue to hunt, even though it becomes very difficult to find food.

MOTHERS AND BABIES

Polar bears mate in the spring. The male and female polar bears only stay together for a few days or weeks after they have mated. The babies are born eight to nine months later. Polar bear mothers raise their young alone.

The pregnant bears travel to special areas in the Arctic to have their babies. One of the largest known areas is on Wrangel Island in the USSR. Most years over 150 bears go there to have their babies.

Pregnant polar bears make themselves homes called dens in the snow. These are like caves dug out of the icy ground, with tunneled entrances leading to small living quarters.

Polar bears can have up to four babies at a time, but usually they have two. The babies are called cubs. They drink a rich milk from their mother's breasts which gives them all the energy they need to grow. The new families stay inside for most of the winter, unless their dens are damaged in a storm. If this happens, the mother has to find a new place to keep her cubs, carrying them in her teeth if they are too young to walk.

CUB FACTS

When the polar bear cub is born, it is less than half the size of a pet cat. It cannot see or hear. Its body is covered in very short white hairs, but it has no body fat.

When the cub is 26 days old, its ears open and it can hear. When the cub is 33 days old, its eyes open.

After two months, polar bear cubs begin to move around the den.

Three months after being born, the polar bear cubs leave their winter den.

▲ A polar bear mother sits patiently while her cubs are feeding. Her breast milk tastes like cod liver oil and it is as rich as cream. Only seals and some whales have richer milk to offer their babies. While feeding, the cubs may make a soft gurgling noise.

► Polar bear families have to travel vast distances across the 'ice and snow to reach their feeding grounds when they leave their winter dens. They may stop to rest frequently. The young cubs stay close to their mother's body for warmth and comfort.

THE EARLY YEARS

In March, polar bear families leave their winter dens. The mothers are weak and hungry because they have not eaten for over four months. The cubs have been drinking their mother's milk and they are fat and healthy.

For the first year, the cubs stay close to their mother's side. Young cubs have been seen clinging to their mother's back when she is running. Sometimes they hold on to her tail or fur while they are learning to swim. Polar bear families stay together for at least two years.

The mothers start hunting as soon as they reach the pack ice. They may kill more seals than their families can eat so that the cubs can learn their hunting techniques.

Polar bear mothers are fiercely protective. They will stand up to male bears twice their size to protect their cubs. Polar bears "talk" to each other using low growls and hisses. They also use body language such as lowering their heads to show aggression. When polar bears meet, they circle each other suspiciously. If they recognize each other, they gently grasp each other's jaws as a form of greeting.

Polar bears usually live between 15 and 40 years in the wild, but in zoos they can live longer. Many polar bears become very unhappy when kept in captivity because they do not have enough living space. In the wild, polar bears can travel hundreds of kilometers every week.

◀ Polar bear mothers help their cubs learn to swim, often getting behind and gently pushing them on when they become tired. This young cub has just had a swimming lesson.

▶ Polar bear mothers are very attentive and never let their cubs out of sight. Even when danger approaches, they will not desert their young cubs.

FINDING FOOD

Polar bears are expert hunters. They have good eyesight and excellent hearing. They have an incredible sense of smell which allows them to sniff out food over 32 kilometers (20 miles) away.

Polar bears can move without a sound thanks to their thick, furry paws. Their white coloring makes them difficult to see on the ice.

Although adult bears hunt alone, many bears may gather for a large

HUNTING FACTS

Polar bears break into seal dens by stamping on the icy den roofs with their mighty paws.

If they have to swim to reach their prey, polar bears slip into the water hind paws first so as not to make a sound.

meal. Over 30 polar bears have been seen feasting together on a whale carcass.

Polar bears are very strong. They can kill seals with one swift paw movement and may break the seals' bones as they drag them through the ice.

Polar bears are very clean creatures. After every meal they lick themselves clean and roll in the snow. If there is water nearby, they may wash.

◀ When polar bears are thirsty, they gnaw the ice to get drinking water.

▲ The polar bear's sense of smell is very powerful. They can track down a meal many kilometers away. Scientists working in the Arctic report that when they cook their meals, bears appear within minutes as if from nowhere.

▶ Away from their hunting grounds, polar bears survive by eating grass, berries and seaweed, and catching small mammals and birds. Some bears travel inland to raid cabins or scavenge in garbage dumps.

NEIGHBORS

Very few people live near the Arctic, but polar bears share their home with lots of other animals which have also learned to live in the icy climate.

Packs of Arctic foxes often follow polar bears long distances. When a bear makes a kill, the foxes wait nearby for it to finish its meal and pick up any scraps that have been left behind.

There are lots of different animals living in the icy Arctic waters, including ringed seals – the polar bear's favorite food. Ringed seals have a very strong body smell and bad breath. This makes them easy for polar bears to track down. Seals are excellent swimmers, but they are slow and clumsy on land.

The only animal that can be a

danger to the polar bear is the fearsome walrus, with its long, white tusks. Like ringed seals, walruses are clumsy on land but good swimmers. When a walrus is swimming nearby, polar bears will not enter the water.

Some whales, such as belugas and narwhals, can be found in the Arctic Ocean. Polar bears have been known to catch small whales and pull them out of the water when they are trapped by ice.

Some birds like snowy owls and ducks live in the Arctic permanently, and large flocks of birds visit the area to breed and raise their young. The most famous visitor is the Arctic tern which travels from the Arctic to the Antarctic and back again every year – a longer migration than any other living creature.

▲ Arctic foxes hunt lemmings and other small mammals when they are not scavenging from the polar bears.

◀ Large flocks of birds, such as the guillemots in this picture, lay their eggs on the rocky Arctic coasts. Guillemots produce colorful eggs that will not roll off the cliff edge.

▶ The walrus is a member of the seal family. It is the only seal that grows long, white tusks. Polar bears have been known to kill small walruses for food, but they steer clear of large adults.

THE POLAR BEAR CAPITAL

The town of Churchill in the Canadian Arctic is visited by polar bears every year. It has been called the 'polar bear capital of the world'. Children in Churchill are taught bear safety in schools.

Polar bears go to Churchill when they are forced ashore during the summer months. They visit the town to look for food, and leave when the pack ice forms on the Arctic waters again.

For many years people and bears tolerated each other. Nowadays, if the bears go into town they are tranquilized and then flown back to the wild. Visitors to Churchill are taken across the icy land in planes and giant buggies to see the polar bears.

POLAR BEAR FACTS

Wooden cabins are often raided by polar bears. They break down doors and smash through walls to get to the food stored inside.

◀ Bears are lured to garbage dumps in Churchill by the smell of rotting food. The town has tried to stop the bears from visiting the dumps, but nothing seems to put them off. Polar bears will even rummage through burning garbage, so desperate are they for scraps of food.

MAN – FRIEND OR FOE?

In the 1950s, hunting polar bears became a fashionable "sport". Small planes were flown over the bears' icy home and the hunters shot them from the air. Russia banned the killing of bears in 1957, but elsewhere hunting continued. It was estimated that in 1965 alone about 1500 bears were killed.

Polar bears do not belong to any one country. They may travel through Alaska, Canada, Norway, Greenland and the USSR. International meetings had to take place to decide the fate of the polar bear.

In 1975, a worldwide agreement was made. It allowed local people to hunt a limited number of bears in the traditional manner for food and clothing. Hunting by air was banned.

Polar bears have been saved from hunters with planes and guns, but they now have to share their home with oil and mining companies. Some polar bear experts believe that these developments once again threaten the polar bears' existence.

▼ In the 1970s, world attention focused on the polar bears and an international agreement was reached to save them from the hunters' guns.

POLAR BEAR MASK

Try making a mask. You will need a piece of cardboard or thick paper, a length of elastic or string, and a pair of scissors.

Draw the basic mask shape onto the cardboard. Remember to make two holes for your eyes and a small hole at each side of the mask. Carefully cut out your mask shape and then decide how you are going to decorate it. When your mask is decorated, thread the elastic or string through the two holes at the side of the mask.

There are lots of ways to decorate masks. Here are a few things to try.

crayons

yarn

paint

fabric

colored paper

◀ Our mask was made by cutting out this basic shape from cardboard and covering it with fabric.

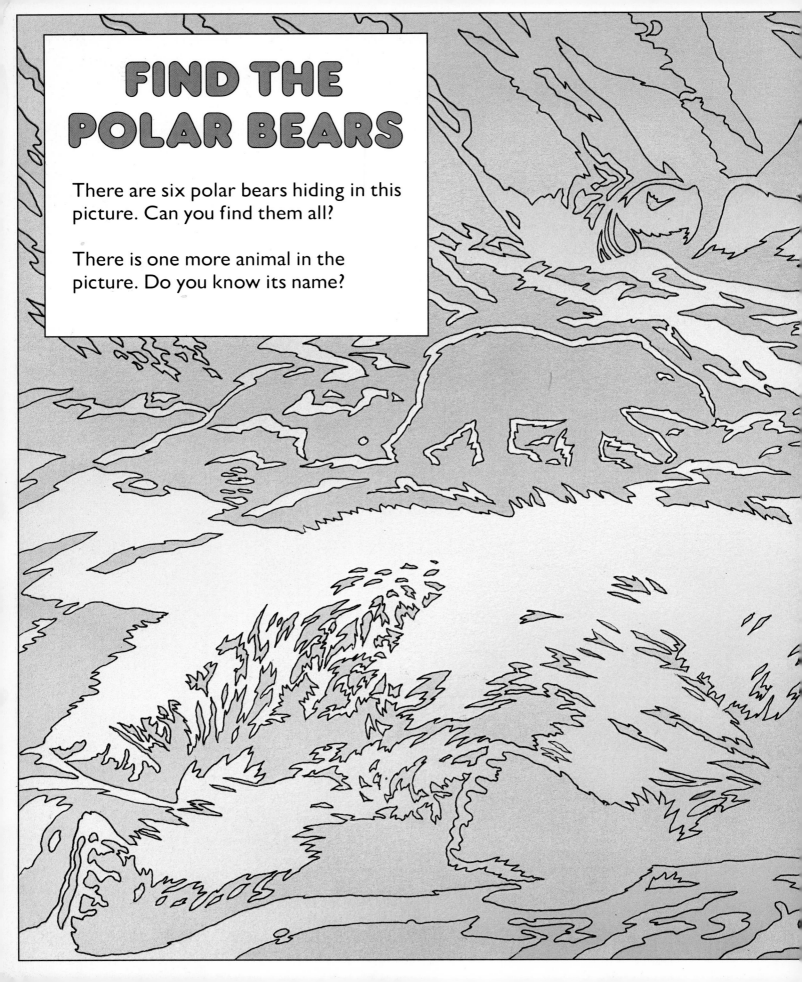

FIND THE POLAR BEARS

There are six polar bears hiding in this picture. Can you find them all?

There is one more animal in the picture. Do you know its name?

PREPARING FOR WINTER

BY ROBIN KINGSLAND

The great white she-bear stopped at the water's edge. She rose up onto her hind legs, lifted her nose high and stood motionless, sniffing the freezing Arctic air. There were seals close by. She looked around slowly, careful not to frighten her prey with a sudden movement.

Winter was nearly upon her and the white she-bear had lots to do. The cubs she carried inside her body would need shelter and support. She must go to her denning area and build a home for them. But first, she had to eat. The great white she-bear was very hungry.

Something caught her eye at the far edge of the stretch of water, a flash of sunlight, a sprinkling of tiny silver flashes as something disturbed the surface – it was a seal. More important, it was food!

Perhaps it was not alone; perhaps it had a lair somewhere near, thought the she-bear as she slid hind first into the chilly water. No splash – only a gently widening, soundless ripple.

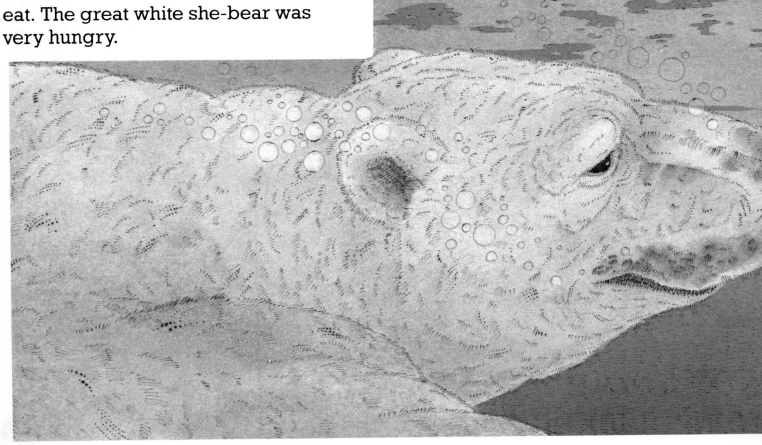

Flattening her ears against her head and closing her nostrils, she pushed through the water. She swam strongly and quickly, moving more gracefully in water than she lumbered on land.

Fast as she was, though, the seal was faster. Some instinct had told it that danger was near. Long before the she-bear reached it, the seal saw her. With a muscular thrashing beat of its tail the seal shot through icy, green water. The bear pressed after it. As the distance closed the she-bear was sure that her prey was almost caught.

Then, quite suddenly, with a cunning flick and twist, the seal changed direction and disappeared into an ice crevice.

With all the speed she could muster, the she-bear threw herself out of the water and began to peer through the ice for signs of the seal. Perhaps its lair was here, under the surface. If so, one stamp of her hind feet or one shattering blow of her paws would expose it and her hunt would be over.

For some minutes she searched, but there was neither sign nor scent. The seal had gone.

The she-bear shook herself, sending a high curving spray of icy drops into the air. If only she had been quicker, or the seal slower. If only the seal had not turned and seen her. If only . . .

In spite of the cold, the she-bear rose again, her tall body creamy-white against the sky. Again she breathed deeply, her fine sense of smell ready to pick up any scent. Then it was there. That strange, oily scent of men and machines. It was far away, perhaps a dozen or twenty miles, but somewhere there was a man-camp. And where there was a man-camp, there was food. In store huts or in among the rubbish bins, there would be food. At any other time, she would have avoided the men, not liking their bright lights and the heat of their machinery, but hunger drove her on.

At the man-camp, they saw her coming. No one tried to stop her. They could see that she was in need of food. If she went near the stores they could frighten her away, but she headed for the bins. She would make a mess, but she would do no damage.

"Wow," said one of the men, "Just like Goldilocks."

"Only this time, Mama bear's stealing the porridge!" said another, and they watched as she waded through the rubbish in the great bins, looking for something, anything, that would see her through the winter.

In her desperate search for food, the she-bear had come many miles out of her way. She had traveled in a huge half-circle to reach the man-camp. Now, having eaten a little of the men's leftovers, she decided to head straight across the ice for her denning site. She began her journey knowing, with an animal's sense, which way she wanted to go. She was still hungry, but she must hurry to prepare a winter den before her cubs were born.

The she-bear was making steady progress when, suddenly, she stopped and lifted her head. She could smell fresh meat. Hungry and excited, she followed her nose ...

As she got near, another smell reached her. The smell of other bears, lots of them. She moved faster and faster, throwing herself up a slope of ice. With a roar of greeting and relief, she reached the crest of the hill. Below her – a beached whale.

The whale was dead, killed by men in their boats or stranded by an unusual tide. It didn't matter. It was food now. A polar bear feast before the bitterest deep of winter. Males, females, and young would be able to eat their fill.

The great white she-bear began to lope towards the group, picking up speed down the slope as the whale smell grew stronger in her nostrils. Now she had nothing to fear. Here was all the food she would need. Enough to survive the coldest months and give her the reserves she would need to feed her cubs.

As the polar wind hummed across the ice, the she-bear reached the group and began to eat.

TRUE OR FALSE ?

Which of these facts are true and which ones are false? If you have read this book carefully, you will know the answers.

1. Polar bears are larger than lions and tigers.
2. Polar bears have long legs and short necks.
3. Inuits hunt polar bears for food and clothing.
4. Polar bears dig caves in the snow during the Arctic winter.
5. Summer is the best hunting time for polar bears.

6. Polar bears hunt in large groups.
7. Polar bears have a poor sense of smell.
8. Polar bears swim on their backs.

9. Polar bears clean themselves regularly.

10. Polar bears eat grasses and berries during the Arctic winter.
11. Polar bear cubs are born with no fur on their bodies.

12. Polar bear cubs sometimes ride on their mother's back.
13. Polar bear mothers will stand up to male bears twice their size to protect their cubs.
14. Polar bears mate for life.
15. Churchill, Canada, is known as the polar bear capital of the world.